MW01121006

Prologue
(that's the bit before the story)

You find yourself staring at a group of people who are staring at someone else.

Who are they staring at?

Why are they staring?

Are the people they are staring at staring back at them? Is this whole book just a giant staring contest?

The people staring definitely look **excited** and like they are anticipating something. So you know the thing they're staring at is **SPECTACULAR.**

Or maybe not-so-**SPECTACULAR,** but they feel like they have to keep looking.

To figure out what they are staring at and if you, too, should stare, start reading!

An adventure awaits!

Whoa! What a drumroll! Usually, a drumroll is greeted with delight. It means something wonderful is about to happen. It means that something is so worthy of a drumroll—*so dependent on that roll of the drum*—that the thing can't even *think* about beginning before you hear that **da-da-da-da-da-da.**

Or whatever sound a drum makes.

But this drumroll is greeted with **ANGER.** What is about to happen? It seems like those kids are going to do something that is so special that it requires a drumroll.

But, to find out what *is* so worthy of a drumroll, you'll have to read the backstory.

> Psst, you— yes, you!—pay attention to the pink words.

And you probably won't really want to do it. But, we promise, you'll be happy that you did.

So, without further ado … **drumroll, please!**

Backstory

This is **Perri Petunia III**—those lines mean "the third." She is twelve years old. She insists on saying twelve and three-quarters. She likes reading. But she only says that to adults because they like to hear things like that. She prefers going on adventures with her brother, Archer. And playing softball.

This is **Archer.** He is nine. He's crazy about danger and adventure. He likes going on adventures to find his favorite things: pizza, goofy objects, and maps. He hates adventures that lead him to his least favorite things: vegetables, vegetables, and vegetables. He lettuce know that he really hates vegetables.

Yep, more backstory (sigh)

A lifetime ago, when she was seven years old, Eliza Effervescent—Aunt Bubbles to Perri and Archer—found a black silky hat that looked like a chimney pot. It kindled her love of collecting. Her wacky world of wonders began as a modest shack of shocking souvenirs. Then it morphed into a maze of mysteries until, finally, its size challenged the finest hotels in the world. It needed a new name—**Lost & Found: The Effervescent Emporium of Curiosities.**

⟵ This is Aunt Bubbles, donning her Teasmaid Hat*

*patent pending

10

Even more backstory?! When will it end?!

Short story long: One of the most special, fantastic, un-be-*lieve*-able treasures arrived only two years ago. The story begins as most great stories do: It was a dark and stormy night. A woman hooked and crooked like a question mark entered Lost & Found. She opened a velvet box and bestowed a magical gift on Perri and Archer—a set of books that allowed them to travel through time. She said, "The pages of *The World Book* will flutter. The old grandmother clock will

BRONG and BRONG.

Delicate bubbles will ooze from the clock's face. Lost & Found will fade away, and your adventure will begin."

Short story shorter: A bent woman gave two kids a time-traveling device.

chapter 1: Was that worth a drumroll? We think so.

"To be bored, or not to be bored," Archer **sighed.** A heatwave limited Perri and Archer to an inside activity.

It was Perri's turn to **sigh.** "Softball is certainly out, but I'll think of something for us to do. Hey, isn't what you just said a famous line from a play or something?" Perri asked.

Archer shook his head. "Not a play—a restaurant. That burrito place Aunt Bubbles took us: To Bean or Not to Bean."

"Oh, right. The place where the beans were optional," Perri clarified. "Well, maybe we could play something. Like when we were younger and would play doctor or school. Or play Olympics."

"We could play restaurant," Archer suggested. He flipped his palm up to face the ceiling and pretended to swirl between tables, like a graceful waiter. He stood as **STRAIGHT** as if he was glued to a flagpole. "Beans or no beans today, madam?"

Perri had an idea percolating.

Drip, drip, drip.

"Or how about play play?" Perri suggested.

"Play play? What's that?" Archer asked.

"Well, I guess just *put on* a play. We could write,

direct, produce, and act in our own play. Like Aunt Bubbles said she used to do with her childhood friend."

"What was his name again?"

"Billy Shakespeare," Perri said.

"That's right. What would the play be about?" Archer inquired, warming up to the idea. He threw his imaginary tray to the ground, breaking plates and chalices. He removed his imaginary tuxedo.

"Well, there are lots of options. We could do a drama or a comedy. It could be about our time-traveling adventures."

"Oooo I like this idea," Archer said. "I think we could make a play about an old, crooked woman shaped like a question mark. She could present these two incredible, amazing, brilliant children with a collection of books. The books then transport these fantastic kids to faraway lands. Then they learn about cultures and meet incredible people," Archer said.

"Arch, that's **_our_** story."

"And it's a good one," he said. **"Inspired by true events!"**

"How about we go to the Colossal Cave of Costumes to get some inspiration. Then we can stop by the Awesome Anteroom of Acting Accessories to get some bells and whistles. Every good play needs good bells and whistles," Perri said, already walking

through Lost & Found.

To get some extra rehearsal time in to fine-tune their stage presence, Perri and Archer sped through Lost & Found. They were **MOVING AS QUICKLY** as if they were skating on phonebooks pulled by speedy mice. They imagined themselves performing on a hallowed stage. After their splendid performance, they would savor the applause, the audience, the achievement.

When Perri and Archer reached the Cave of Costumes, they were **delighted** to see such **wonderful** clothes! There were costumes for every play they could imagine.

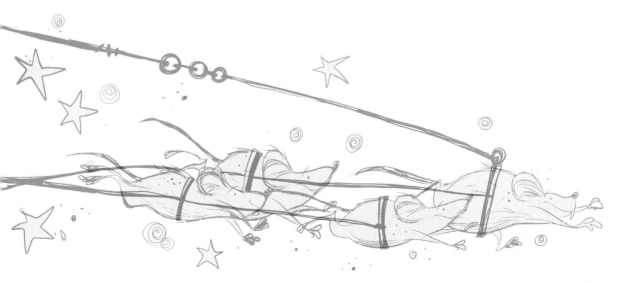

Tutus and robes and armor and stockings and little shoes with bells on the end coated the room. A stuffed giraffe was wearing a Victorian-style wig. The giraffe was named Annabel.

Perri and Archer tried on many outfits before settling on silk robes with **delicate** flowers. Cowboy hats sat atop their heads. Perri carefully removed several strands of carved beads from a massive statue of Buddha and wrapped them around her equally **massive** hat.

Satisfied with their outfits, they made their way to the Awesome Anteroom of Acting Accessories. They had chosen this room, because, as Perri says, "Every good play needs good bells and whistles." And they did, in fact, find bells and whistles.

Archer was rummaging through a large chest searching for a wand when he pulled out something that felt nothing like a wand.

"What is…this?" Archer said, carefully removing

the mysterious object from the chest.

"Perri! Come help!"

Perri *glided* over—she felt like she needed more rehearsal time for a play-worthy walk—and nearly **tripped** over marbles making an escape from the ancient chest and rolling across the floor.

She lifted a director's chair, a prop umbrella, and a few remaining marbles off of the mysterious object.

"I have no idea what this is," Perri said, running her hands along the **delicate** grooves.

"But I sure know that it looks *dainty* and *fragile,*" Archer said. He put his face up to the object and looked through the miniature windows.

"It kind of looks like a doily. Or like a big flag for a party."

"Well, I would say that we should consult *The World Book*. But we wouldn't even know where to begin," Archer said.

Perri and Archer slowly stood up and held the object with o u t s t r e t c h e d arms. They tilted the cowboy hats to the back of their heads, so their impaired vision would not cause them to rumple the beautiful mystery.

"Maybe Aunt Bubbles will know?" Perri asked. "She *is* old enough to know a little bit about pretty much everything that's ever happened in the world."

"Good idea," Archer confirmed.

Perri and Archer inched through Lost & Found in search of Aunt Bubbles.

"Thank goodness we practiced our most *elegant* walks before we found this," Archer said, holding his head high.

"You're right, Arch. Plus, we can count this as an extra rehearsal," Perri said.

An hour later, Perri and Archer reached Aunt Bubbles. It is a rather large space.

"Aunt Bubbles," Archer said, "what is this?"

Aunt Bubbles looked up from her pottery wheel. She **gasped.**

"Where did you find that? Oh, how I've missed it."

She wiped the wet clay on her clothes and rinsed her hands in the pineapple-shaped sink.

She held the object high, e x t e n d i n g her arms so she could take it all in. Perri and Archer shook their arms out—it was exhausting to carry that thing for seemingly miles!

"This is a shadow puppet. It's from Thailand," Aunt Bubbles explained.

"A shadow puppet? But it doesn't look like any puppet I've ever seen," Perri said. "I think of puppets having strings and wooden arms and legs. And they have big, painted eyes that never close."

"Well, yes, some puppets *do* look like that. But not all," Aunt Bubbles said.

"Where is Thailand?" Archer asked. Because he loved maps, he was always eager to learn about the origins of Lost & Found's many, many treasures.

"It is a country in southeast Asia. I grew up th—"
Aunt Bubbles was interrupted. Her pottery wheel
was **spinning** dangerously. Bits of clay flew in every
direction. While she ran to put an end to the
chaos, Perri and
Archer carefully
took the
puppet.

They went to consult their trusted guide: *The World Book.*

Once they found the cart on which *The World Book* was proudly displayed, Perri and Archer found the "T" volume. They turned to "Thailand."

Archer read, "'Thailand is a country in tropical Southeast Asia. The people of Thailand are called Thai.' Hmm, this is interesting: 'For most of its history, the country was called Siam. In 1939, it officially adopted the name Thailand.'"

"I wonder why that is," Perri said. "Aunt Bubbles changed her name. But she probably did it in 1399."

Perri and Archer read through "Recreation," "Languages," and "Food."

"I'm glad their food isn't hardtack," Archer said, recoiling and shuddering. He'd eaten hardtack on a recent time-traveling adventure. He would *not* be eating it again.

Perri nodded. She kept reading, "'The arts in Thailand are greatly influenced by Buddhism. Buddhist temples display some of the finest Thai architecture. The image of Buddha appears in many Thai paintings and sculptures. Modern Thai painting features traditional religious themes and international styles.'"

Archer continued reading, "'Some dramas were shadow plays performed with puppets.'"

BRONG

BRONG

BRONG

"Perri! The **BRONGS** are here—we are going on an adventure!" Archer squealed.

"Quick—"

BRONG

"Get something to put this in. It's so **beautiful** and delicate. I don't want to ruin it," Perri said. She frantically searched through a bag of other, smaller bags. She extracted a weathered, leather briefcase from the grasp of Aunt Bubbles's octopus bag.

Perri and Archer hastily removed their silk robes and cowboy hats. Although they were in a hurry to get on with their adventure, they neatly folded their silk robes.

They did, however, toss their cowboy hats into the sky.

Luckily, they landed on hat stands.

Perri carefully placed the Thai shadow puppet in

the briefcase. Just as she snapped the lock, bubbles started floating from the old grandmother clock—the one that was hooked and crooked like a question mark.

The World Book started *fluttering* its pages.

Flip flip flip

Flip flip flip

BRONG

BRONG

BRONG

"Ready, Arch?" Perri asked, tightening her grip on the briefcase. She checked the lock one more time to make sure they had the puppet.

"Ready!" Archer **SHRIEKED.**

Perri and Archer floated through time!

They somersaulted and cartwheeled past centuries and decades.